21-DAY DEVOTIONAL

Climbing Out of The Past & Reaching For the Future

The OUTCOME

ANDRE LOVE-HOSEA

The Outcome: 21-Day Devotional

Copyright © 2020 Andre Love-Hosea

Unless otherwise noted, all Bible quotations are from the King James Version of the Bible.

Cover Design, Typesetting, Book Layout by
Enger Lanier Taylor for In Due Season Publishing

Published By: In Due Season Publishing
               Huntsville, Alabama
               indueseasonpublishing@gmail.com
               www.indueseasonpublishing.com

ISBN-13:   978-1-970057-09-6
ISBN-10:   1-970057-09-2

Instagram: @thatwaydre
Twitter: @whoischamptv
www.drejose.com

CONTENTS

Introduction

Waking up is the most incredible privilege that we receive as humans, but when we start our day, we forget to thank God for opening our eyes. Social media will always be there, your surroundings will always be there, but we must understand that seeing the next twenty hours is a blessing.

For the next 21 days, dedicate time just for you and God. Whether this maybe when you wake up, before bed, or noonday, after you have an official time, choose a place where you will not be distracted or hear your phone ringing. Once that is done, you are now officially set to read, pray, and listen. Listening to God the next 21 days will be critical, and as Habakkuk 2:2 states, "And the Lord answered me, and said, Write the vision, and make it plain upon tables, that he may run that readeth it."

Write down your affirmations each day and watch God work!

DAY 1

Being Firm

In October, trees begin to lose their leaves, and when the humidity is high, they also lose their branches. When a storm comes, trees start to shake and make noises, but trees will always stand their ground no matter what is happening.

In my grandmother's yard, there were trees of all sizes. I mean, there wasn't any grass in her yard, just dirt, and trees. The trees were so firm. I didn't think anything could take them out. While a branch or two may have hit the ground, the trees were so old they refused to be knocked down by a storm.

It's easy to stand tall and be firm when nothing is coming your way, but how do you react when a storm hits your life? Are you standing like a tree, or did you give up when life smacked you in the face? A tree has faced many storms, and although branches fell, and it may have cracked a little, they still held on. Standing firm means to hold on to God's Word. I can guarantee you that if you haven't already faced a storm, you will. None of us are exempt. We have all heard that "Pressure breaks pipes." Will you be broken like a pipe or stand your ground like a tree when that storm comes?

During the storm, you will crack, you may even want to throw in the towel, but will you plant your feet into his Word and stand tall? That is what going and growing through a storm is, knowing that one will come, but having no worries concerning them.

Verse of the Day: *That person is like a tree planted by streams of water, which yields its fruit in season and whose leaf does not wither whatever they do prospers.* **Psalm 1:3**

Question of the Day: How have you handled the previous storms of your life?

_____

_____

Are you standing firm in God's Word?

_____

_____

_____

_____

_____

_____

_____

_____

_____

_____

_____

_____

_____

_____

_____

_____

_____

_____

_____

_____

_____

_____

_____

_____

_____

_____

_____

_____

<u>Daily Affirmation:</u>

_____

_____

_____

_____

_____

_____

_____

_____

_____

_____

_____

_____

_____

_____

_____

_____

_____

_____

_____

_____

_____

_____

_____

_____

DAY 2

Half Full / Half Empty

Someone once asked me, "Would I prefer to be half-full or half-empty." For a second, I didn't understand, but the logic is that if things aren't going your way, you only see the bad and begin to stress instead of knowing that better days are to come.

Some people wake up on top of the world, and within a few short minutes, the world is on top of them. Having the right perception is the key to understanding every situation and knowing how to adjust to it properly. Think about an incident that has happened thus far, and write the outcome of that situation. During those times, what did you learn from it, and did it make a positive impact? Most times, we tend to overlook the good because we are so focused on the bad.

In all truthfulness, the answer is entirely up to you, whether you are half-full or half-empty. While being asked the most straightforward questions, our mind tends to wander the most. Not once do we insert God in the perspective, we never stop and ask ourselves what God is trying to show us at that moment. You must remove your thought process from the earth and view things from the spirit past the present moment. Next time you face opposition, don't become angry; instead, simply smile, knowing that things will get better.

Verse of the Day:
Trust in the LORD with all your heart and lean not on your own understanding; in all your ways submit to him, and he will make your paths straight. **Proverbs 3:5-6 NIV**

Question: Are you living as half-full or half-empty?

_____

_____

_____

_____

_____

_____

Daily Affirmation:

_____

_____

_____

_____

_____

_____

_____

_____

_____

_____

_____

_____

_____

_____

_____

_____

_____

_____

_____

_____

_____

_____

_____

DAY 3

Forgiveness is Key

Forgiveness is defined as a deliberate decision to release feelings of resentment or vengeance toward a person or group who may have harmed you. Regardless of whether they deserve your forgiveness or not, it can be a tough thing to do. Maybe someone has betrayed and hurt you to the core. Forgiveness does not mean that you weren't affected by the situation or that you don't blame the other person. Often you hear, "forgive and forget," but just because you forgive does not mean you now have amnesia. It means that you are no longer held captive by that memory.

Even when you thought that you had forgiven the person, there is always going to be something attacking that may cause you to realize that the situation is well and alive. Forgiveness is about you setting yourself free. There is only one person who's controlling your freedom, and that is you. You are locking yourself in a cell. Not being able to forgive someone causes damage to the body, and you may be angry at everyone who doesn't deserve it. Ephesians 4: 31-32 states, "Get rid of all bitterness, rage, and anger, brawling, and slander, along with every form of malice. be kind and compassionate to one another, forgiving each other, just as in Christ God forgave you."

To forgive means that you are letting go of all of the pain that the incident caused you no matter what it may take. The situation doesn't fall on you, but how you react to it does. You will never be able to give 100% in your current relationship if you haven't forgiven your previous partner for hurting you. Maybe your mother or father hurt you; not forgiving your parents for the hurt that was caused could potentially affect the relationship with your children.

You may say that you are who you are today because of what transpired in your life and how people treated you, but God lets us know that your past has does not have to have control over your present and will have no power over the places you are going. If you are faithful and willing to forgive others, God promised that He would forgive you.

Verse of the Day: *Get rid of all bitterness, rage and anger, brawling and slander, along with every form of malice. Be kind and compassionate to one another, forgiving each other, just as in Christ God forgave you.* **Ephesians 4: 31-32**

Question of the Day: If God forgave you, what stops you from forgiving those who caused you pain?

_____

_____

_____

_____

_____

_____

_____

_____

_____

_____

_____

_____

_____

_____

Daily Affirmation:

_____

_____

_____

_____

_____

_____

_____

_____

_____

_____

_____

_____

_____

_____

_____

_____

_____

_____

_____

_____

_____

_____

DAY 4

The Art of Fruitfulness

Have you ever come so close to quitting, but stayed in the race and was rewarded the benefits? If I told you that the blessing you have been praying for was on the other side of that wall, would you knock it down no matter what it takes? Most times, we quit right before the blessing arrives. Have you ever given up and immediately regretted it? God never gave up on you, so why should we, as His children, do something that He has never done?

You must be fruitful before you can do anything. In other words, you have to go through something to grow through something. "A job is a job" we have all heard that one, right? I have witnessed people quit their job because it wasn't paying what they imagined. Know your worth! Yes, this is true, but to be honest, if God placed you at that current job on that pay scale, it is for a reason. If you stay the course, He guaranteed us that we would reap if we do not faint.

A decade ago, when I began to cut hair, I did it for free for more than seven years. I found myself quitting my job because my passion was to make people feel good and smile, although I was not getting paid for it. During those tough times, when I had no income, I still managed to wake up before sunrise and cut hair for free. There were days when I was broke, but God made a promise that if I did not give up, that I would reap the reward. God said we have to be fruitful before we can multiply. He won't bless you with ten thousand dollars if you don't know how to handle one-hundred dollars properly. Maybe you haven't gotten that general manager position because you are still learning as a sales associate. Keep pushing forward no matter what your pay grade currently may be. Remember, it's never about your skill; it's your will. Trust that the place that you are in now are only stepping stones for the things to come.

Verse of the Day: *God blessed them and said to them, "Be fruitful and increase in number; fill the* *earth and subdue it. Rule over the fish of the sea and the birds of the air and over every living creature that moves on the ground.* **Genesis 1:28**

<u>Question of the Day</u>: Where are you giving up in life? Have you ever giving up and immediately regretted it?

_____

_____

_____

_____

_____

_____

_____

_____

_____

_____

_____

_____

_____

_____

_____

_____

_____

_____

_____

_____

Daily Affirmation:

DAY 5

Snooze or Wake Up

Have you ever been so tired that even after a full eight hours of rest, you still need to sleep some more?

While training for the U.S. Army in Fort Jackson, SC, during the summer of 2019, I was getting the best sleep of my life. My alarm went off at 5:15 A.M. for physical training (PT) that consisted of running, push-ups, and other workouts the instructor had planned. I quickly hit the snooze button, not realizing that time would pass as fast as it came. I found myself to be the last officer in formation. That struck a nerve with me and made me angry at myself for hitting snooze.

Some of us are not just hitting snooze on our alarm, but we are hitting it in other aspects of life.

Maybe you have been hitting snooze on your dreams, goals, or even the purpose God has for you.

Take a couple of minutes out of your day and ask yourself, "While I'm sleeping, what is everyone else around me doing." The thing about life is that it will go on with or without you; the choice is yours. The results you get will be from the work that you put in. Nothing will come to a person who rests all day. Eventually, you have to decide whether you'll continue to hit snooze or wake up. The truth of the matter is that when you hit snooze, you are telling God, no! Maybe He's been calling you to do some things, but you are saying, "Maybe tomorrow, I'm not ready today." Do not allow life to continue passing you by; there's no better time than now!

Verse of The Day: *Do not love sleep or you will grow poor; stay awake and you will have food to spare.* **Proverbs 20:13**

Question: Will you continue to hit snooze on life or decide to wake up and get the advantage? Identify where you are hitting the snooze button?

_____

ANDRE LOVE-HOSEA

Daily Affirmation:

_____

_____

_____

_____

_____

_____

_____

_____

_____

_____

_____

_____

_____

_____

_____

_____

_____

_____

_____

_____

_____

_____

_____

_____

_____

_____

_____

_____

_____

DAY 6

Plans & Purpose

Have you ever made plans, but unfortunately, things didn't go your way? Or expected one thing and received another? Of course, we have all made plans at one point, and they failed. Maybe you made plans to be at work at 7:00 A.M., but traffic was so bad that you didn't arrive until 7:45 A.M. You didn't realize how God just saved you from that accident that happened. So just be patient and fulfill the purpose that He has set inside of you.

We never acknowledge that our purpose is much larger than we can ever imagine. Maybe you are reading this and have no idea how great your purpose truly is. There may have been a tragic event in your life, and you are feeling down and sorry for yourself. There's no doubt in my mind that your tragic event happened to bring you closer to your purpose or the reason you lost your job was because you were complacent with that paycheck instead of taking a leap of faith. You made plans to retire from that job, knowing that you should be the employer instead of the employee.

Years ago, someone suggested I make a 5-year plan, and in that plan, I would include my goals from finances, relationships, school, and business. One month after creating my plan, it seems as if everything on my list had shattered. My business hit an all-time low, and the things I thought I had control of I did not. I was told to make that 5-year plan about everything I wanted, but no one told me to put God in the center of it. Now is the time to prepare for the things and purpose that God has for you. I challenge you to write a 5-year plan and put God in the center of it and watch it reveal itself to you.

Verse of the Day: *And we know that in all things God works for the good of those who love him, who have been called according to his purpose.* **Romans 8:28**

<u>Question of the Day</u>: Are your plans tied to your purpose/ If so, how?

_____

_____

_____

_____

_____

_____

_____

_____

_____

_____

_____

_____

_____

_____

_____

_____

_____

_____

_____

_____

_____

_____

_____

Daily Affirmation:

DAY 7

Leaving vs. Coming

How many times have you heard or maybe even said, "I came in this world alone, and that's how I'm going to leave?" People say that for different reasons, maybe because at the time they're angry or simply just stating the truth. If this is the case, why do we risk our lives for things we cannot take with us? We are willing to die over clothes, shoes, and money, all materialistic things that have no real value, but we are hurt when we don't get the new pair of shoes.

You may work seven days a week to have a large check, but what would happen if you were to die on your payday? Could you take your money to heaven and ask God to spend it there? When you were born, you came in with nothing, and when you die, it will be the same way. No one will be able to go with you. It doesn't matter the amount of money you have, how many shoes you have, or what type of clothes are in your closet. None of those things will go into consideration for getting you into heaven. You came in with nothing, but leaving with nothing is the biggest mistake. What are you doing now that will matter when everything is said and done? 1 John 2:15 states, "Do not love the world or anything in the world. If anyone loves the world, love for the Father is not in them." In other words, do not love the things that are in the world. Many people praise materialistic things and money, but those things hold no value; instead, be the change and impact someone's life. How would you like to be remembered? It's easy to be talked about while you are here on earth, but once you are gone, how long will that talk continue

Verse of the Day: *For we brought nothing into the world, and we can take nothing out of it.*
1 Timothy 6:7

Question of the Day: What are you doing now that will matter when everything is said and done?

ANDRE LOVE-HOSEA

Daily Affirmation:

_____

_____

_____

_____

_____

_____

_____

_____

_____

_____

_____

_____

_____

_____

_____

_____

_____

_____

_____

_____

_____

_____

_____

DAY 8

Old School Prayer

How do you speak to the father when you pray? Maybe you are like me and wasn't taught a particular way to pray, so you did the traditional thing by getting on your knees and repeating, "Now I lay me down to sleep, I pray the Lord, my soul, to keep, if I should die before I wake, I pray the Lord my soul to take." Don't get me wrong, there is absolutely nothing wrong with that, but when it comes to praying, you to have to talk to God the same way you talk to your parents when you want something. Whether you are in your greatest or darkest days, talk to God because you never want to be the one who only talks to Him in the time of need. You set boundaries on your blessings by asking for things that God has already worked out; now is the time to speak those things that are not as though they were.

I remember going to my mother's church, where the deacons would pray longer than the pastor would preach. The deacons understood there is power in the tongue, and prayer is the key to the future, asking God to do things that only he can do. You have to do an old school prayer at times, go to the end of the bed, get on your knees, and with no distractions, begin to speak everything that comes to your mind.

Are you giving 50 % on your prayer? Do you believe the things you are saying? There's no specific time limit when it comes to praying, but you do want to ensure that God knows you are giving it your all, don't hold back; instead, make your words more powerful than ever. Don't put boundaries on your prayers. If you ask God for an apartment, take it up a level and ask for a home. Go into detail describing the acres of the land and how many bedrooms you would like. Once you have asked now, you must believe and keep the faith knowing it will come.

Verse of the Day: *I have made you a father of many nations." He is our father in the sight of God, in whom he believed—the God who gives life to the*

dead and calls into being things that we are not.
Romans 4:17

Question of the Day: Do you limit yourself when praying?_____

_____

Daily Affirmation:

_____

_____

_____

_____

_____

_____

_____

_____

_____

_____

_____

_____

_____

_____

_____

_____

_____

_____

DAY 9

Drumline

How do you handle stress and depression? Some face it head-on and receive help, while others keep it locked inside so no one will know. If you are the latter personality type, I have advice for you; you are only hurting yourself. Most times, if the people surrounding you know you well enough, they have already picked up on it and may have chosen not to express their observations.

Maybe you are the one going through it or the one watching someone else's silent cry. Most people weren't taught to express their feelings. We were taught to bottle everything up and go about our day. What happened on your best days when those feelings that you thought were sealed away come out? At any given moment, this could take place, and your great day wasn't so great anymore, or your bad day just became the worse day of your life.

Just maybe you are currently in a tough situation, and you don't know whether to turn left or right and because that bottle is inside of you, you have no idea what's next for you in life. Understand that God hears and sees everything you were hiding. Unfortunately, that trick doesn't work with the creator. He desires to help you to maneuver through every challenge

Verse of the Day: *Whether you turn to the right or to the left, your ears will hear a voice behind you, saying, "This is the way; walk in it.* **Isaiah 30:21**

Question of the Day: What's in your bottle? / If your bottle was exposed, how would your life change?

_____
_____
_____
_____
_____
_____
_____

Daily Affirmation:

_____

_____

_____

_____

_____

_____

_____

_____

_____

_____

_____

_____

_____

_____

_____

_____

_____

_____

_____

_____

_____

_____

DAY 10

Inventory

When was the last time you conducted inventory? Inventories are conducted to ensure that the proper supply is accounted for and avoid any over stockings. In 2014, my job would have to do inventories every Saturday morning, count all products from the freezer to things on the floor. Most times, we would find food that wasn't needed any longer due to the previous inventory not being counted correctly.

Maybe you need to do inventory throughout your home. There are things you are collecting for no reason, and because you have had them for a certain period of time, you assume that they have gained some value. Maybe you need to take inventory of your friends and associates who could be holding you back. Don't fall into the trap that just because someone has been with you since the beginning that you feel as if you owe them something. To be honest, we all need to conduct an inventory in places of our lives.

How do we expect God to do what He wants to do if we are holding on to things that He instructed us to get rid of? It's not possible. If the proper inventory is not taken in a timely fashion, something will eventually spoil. If anything comes into contact with the spoiled items, they too will be spoiled. You must understand that if you have a spoiled associate in your circle, they will contact others and spread the germs. Grandma said, "All it takes is one bad apple to spoil the whole bunch."

The first step of inventory is acknowledging that it needs to happen. Start with the areas that you know are not perfect and conduct an inventory in that area. Remove what isn't required in areas where dust or freezer-burnt items live. Acknowledge that you made a few mistakes, but every roadblock also has a detour. It isn't the end! God will make you new and whole again. All you have to do is confess.

Verse of the Day: *If we confess our sins, he is*

faithful and just and will forgive us our sins and purify us from all unrighteousness. **1 John 1:9**

Question of the Day: What are some areas in your life that need an inventory to be conducted? What areas have you cleaned, and how has your life improved?

_____

_____

_____

_____

_____

_____

_____

_____

_____

_____

_____

_____

_____

_____

_____

_____

_____

_____

_____

Daily Affirmation:

_____

_____

_____

_____

_____

_____

_____

_____

_____

_____

_____

_____

_____

_____

_____

_____

_____

_____

_____

_____

_____

_____

_____

DAY 11

Reap the Benefit

Growing up, I would eat fruit, save the seeds, and then dig a hole into my grandmother's yard to plant the seeds. After years of not seeing any results, no one ever told me I was planting seeds incorrectly. The timing must be perfect, must have the correct size containers for the seeds, and fresh soil. I wasn't taught any of this. I assumed that once the seed entered the ground, the rain would hit it, and eventually, I would see the outcome. Light is the number one key to ensuring that you will harvest the thing that you have planted.

Are you properly planting your seeds so that you may reap your benefit? Ensure you have all the right things needed, so you will receive an overflow when it is your season. Growing up, I had no idea of all the key things I was missing, which was why I never saw an outcome. Are you praying once a week and expecting a change? I can guarantee you that nothing will come from it because you aren't planting your seed the correct way.

Consistency is a must when you are planting your seeds. You have to pray and be patient, all while waiting for things to manifest. Don't give up when you begin to think the plant has died but stand firm and push on knowing that at that right moment, you will reap the reward of planting your seed. If you want good in your future, do good now. This is the time to plant seeds in your community and watch God reward you.

Verse of the Day:
I planted the seed, Apollos watered it, but God has been making it grow. So, neither the one who plants nor the one who waters is anything, but only God, who makes things grow. The one who plants and the one who waters have one purpose, and they will each be rewarded according to their labor. For we are co-workers in God's service; you are God's field, God's building.
1 Corinthians 3:6-9

ANDRE LOVE-HOSEA

<u>Question of the Day</u>: What seeds are you planting? Are you planting your seeds correctly?

_____

_____

_____

_____

_____

_____

_____

_____

_____

_____

_____

_____

_____

_____

_____

_____

_____

_____

_____

_____

_____

Daily Affirmation:

_____

_____

_____

_____

_____

_____

_____

_____

_____

_____

_____

_____

_____

_____

_____

_____

_____

_____

_____

_____

_____

_____

DAY 12

Overpacking

Have you ever overpacked? We want to pack our entire closet for a trip that may only be a few days. The bags barely fit in the car afterward, but we continue to stuff items in our suitcase when we may only need two outfits and one pair of shoes.

I recall going on a family trip to Walt Disney World in Orlando, Florida, and bringing hoodies and sweatpants. For a time in the year where nothing but heat flowed throughout the state, I landed in a place where wearing a hoodie could send you to the hospital for a heat stroke, but somehow in my mind, I brought them because "I would rather be safe than a sorry."

How is it that I packed clothes that I didn't need for a state that is simply labeled, "The Sunshine

State?" It's easier to leave it than to bring it. In life, when God is trying to take you places, be careful that you are not overpacking. You want to bring everyone and their baggage. It's dangerous to take everyone around you to a place that is just for you. When you're overpacking, it doesn't have to be materialistic things. You may pack bad habits, but you must leave those bad habits behind to get to that place that God has for you. Acts 7:3 states, "Leave your country and your people,' God said, 'and go to the land I will show you." God is telling Abraham to leave the country and the people he knows, but trust that I will show you the things I have for you. Maybe God is telling you the same thing that he told Abraham to leave your current location and the people you're around. This is a comfort zone for most people, and God wants to get you out of there because that is the only way he can ensure you fulfill his calling.

Verse of the Day: *Then the high priest asked Stephen, "Are these charges true?"* **²** *To this he replied: "Brothers and fathers, listen to me! The God of glory appeared to our father Abraham while he was still in Mesopotamia, before he lived in Harran.* **³** *Leave your country and your people,'*

ANDRE LOVE-HOSEA

God said, 'and go to the land I will show you.
Acts 7 1-3

<u>Question of the Day</u>: What things are you overpacking?

_____

_____

_____

_____

_____

_____

_____

_____

_____

_____

_____

_____

_____

_____

_____

_____

_____

_____

_____

_____

Daily Affirmation:

_____

_____

_____

_____

_____

_____

_____

_____

_____

_____

_____

_____

_____

_____

_____

_____

_____

_____

_____

_____

_____

_____

_____

DAY 13

CPR

When situations occur in our lives and let us down, we sometimes give up, without keeping the faith. There's nothing in life that man controls; God has the final word in everything. How do you handle being denied? You either put your head down and feel bad for yourself or smile and continue to know that just because one person told you, "No," doesn't mean it's over.

You have to apply CPR to that dead situation. How do you apply CPR? Luke 18:27 states, Jesus replied, "What is impossible with man is possible with God." Talk to God because He will ALWAYS keep His promise. Decree life over that "no" until it turns into a "yes." There are times that you should realize that the "no" that you received could be a blessing in disguise. Proverbs 18:21 states, the tongue has the power of life and death, and those who love it will eat its fruit.

Faith makes it possible, so you must speak those things as though they are. Whether it's a job, relationship, family, or the future that concerns you, and you feel as if you're stuck. It's time to restart the plan, start that job or business. No matter how tough it gets, continue to apply CPR to everything you expect to change. Even with no money, you should speak wealth over your life and proceed as if you already have it. If you are expecting wealth, you must leave poor spending habits behind and pick up beneficial ones for a person with money. When manifesting, you must change how you speak to others and change the way you think since this is the only way to awaken that dead situation.

Verse of the Day: Jesus replied, "What is impossible with man is possible with God." **Luke 18:27**

Question of the Day: How do you handle being denied?_____

_____

_____

ANDRE LOVE-HOSEA

Daily Affirmation:

_____

_____

_____

_____

_____

_____

_____

_____

_____

_____

_____

_____

_____

_____

_____

_____

_____

_____

_____

_____

_____

_____

DAY 14

Money/Happiness

If you were offered the ability to triple your current pay if you had to do one thing you hate, would you? Most people would do this without second-guessing it at all. When you wake up, are you excited to return to work, or do you dread the place each time you think about it? Money fills our pockets, but it will never fill our hearts. Day to day, you may go work and anxiously watch the clock until it is time to leave, but when payday arrives, somehow you are one of the happiest people in the world.

Your check can buy you many things, but it will never buy you happiness. That smile that came from seeing the deposit in your bank account was only temporary, and I guarantee you it won't last long.

What do you want in life? The moment you figure that out, your life will change forever. Could you work your current job for the next 20-30 years? If answered, no, then you are not happy where you are. Most jobs require that much time before you can retire. You could spend over half of your life at a place you don't enjoy. For generations, the norm has always been to work a 9-5, go home, sleep, and repeat, but it was rarely said that you should start a business or create multiple streams of income. Many people would never think to ask themselves if they are happy with your job because they have never been taught to think outside the box or that they were capable of accomplishing more.

Money can't purchase things that don't have a price tag. The struggle and grind were costly, and because of it, we were taught some valuable lessons. Some may have struggled more than others. We must admit that our "struggle" made us the people that we are now. Some of the wealthiest people on earth have the most problems. Television displays the glamorous side, but you'll never see the things that are behind the multi-million-dollar house and clothes. Some of the best memories I have came from when I had the least amount of money in my pocket.

At the end of your journey, you can blame no one else for your happiness but yourself. Find out what motivates you and spend the rest of your life doing it. If you are truly happy at your job, you wouldn't consider it a job at all. That motivation and fire you have for it should continue to stay lit, and your happiness will always remain.

Verse of the Day: *Whoever loves money never has enough; whoever loves wealth is never satisfied with their income. This too is meaningless.* **Ecclesiastes 5:10**

Question of the Day: Could you retire from your current job? What do YOU want in life?

_____

_____

_____

_____

_____

_____

_____

_____

Daily Affirmation:

_____

_____

_____

_____

_____

_____

_____

_____

_____

_____

_____

_____

_____

_____

_____

_____

_____

_____

_____

_____

_____

_____

_____

_____

DAY 15

Roller Coaster

Have you ever been in line at the amusement park for a ride, and as you wait, you were nervous but excited at the same time? The thrill of getting on the ride is what makes it worthwhile. Before getting on a roller coaster, you receive many feelings, and once the ride starts, your stomach may drop, and throughout the turns, flips, and fast speed, you may be full of anxiety. But once the roller coaster comes to an end, how do you feel?

Your journey is similar to a roller coaster that comes with many turns, flips, and may flow at a fast pace. You must fasten your seat belt of life and experience the flips and turns that may consist of failure in relationships, business, and friendships, but not all turns are stomach dropping. Amid the thrill, you'll smile, laugh, and kick your feet up, not wanting the ride to end.

What do you do when the thrill is over? You could return from the first ride and choose to get back on the roller coaster and tackle the turns and flips differently. The thrill comes from you feeling a certain way, and at times you may not want to ride it again. You may feel as if the ride is too much, and it's easier to give up before you even get on. Be thankful for the ride. It is the thing that will change your life for the better.

Verse of the Day: I have fought the good fight, I have finished the race, I have kept the faith.
2 Timothy 4:7

Question of the Day: How do you react after the thrill is over?

_____
_____
_____
_____
_____
_____
_____
_____

Daily Affirmation:

_____

_____

_____

_____

_____

_____

_____

_____

_____

_____

_____

_____

_____

_____

_____

_____

_____

_____

_____

_____

_____

_____

DAY 16

Closed Mouths Don't Get Fed

When you are having problems, who do you call? When you were younger and wanted something out of the store, who did you ask? Was it your mother or father? So many times, we have heard, "A closed mouth doesn't get fed." Would you prefer to ask and receive or remain silent and go without? Some would remain silent and not have the blessings that have their names on it, but few ask.

Who do you ask when you want something? Is it your mother or your father because you know they will buy whatever you desire to put a smile on your face? Most people have a favorite parent. Typically, this isn't based on logic but based on which parent spoils you the most. We take everything to our parents from our wants and needs when times get tough and seek them out for a shoulder to cry on. Matthew 7:7 states, "Ask and it will be given to you; seek and you will find; knock and the door will be opened to you. For everyone who asks receives; he who seeks finds; and to him who knocks, the door will be opened." We tend to express our feelings to everyone but God. Friends come and ask you what is wrong, and there is no pressure to explain to them the situation, but we are so quick to ignore God and pretend like He isn't watching. You tell your problems to your mother and father, but not to the great Father above who controls every storm you face.

Why hold back on the things that God already knows? He is waiting for you to confess those things so you may get past them. Converse with God as if He is one of your best friends. Express every thought that appears in your mind and ask for those things that you need.

Verse of the Day: *Ask, and it will be given to you; seek and you will find; knock and the door will be opened to you. For everyone who asks receives; he who seeks finds; and to him who knocks, the door* *will be opened.* **Matthew 7:7**

<u>Question of the Day</u>: Who do you call when you are having problems? Why do you hold things back from God?

_____

_____

_____

_____

_____

_____

_____

_____

_____

_____

_____

_____

_____

_____

_____

_____

_____

_____

_____

Daily Affirmation:

DAY 17

The Know-It-All

We all know one person who thinks they know everything. You can tell them that they are wrong, and they will still debate what you are saying even if you have proof. Know-it-all individuals only see things their way and always want to be the answer to every problem. Imagine going on a road trip, and GPS says to keep ahead 10 miles, but you insist on going with your mind and close out the GPS. Eventually, you end up lost because you decided not to use your resources and listened to yourself; you are frustrated and overwhelmed. Now is the time to utilize the resources that God has made available; no man on earth truly knows it all except for God. How would you feel if God appointed you as the know-it-all for the earth, and every time someone had a question, they were instructed to come to you for answers?

You may think that having something to say about everything makes you look important or indispensable. Unfortunately, being labeled as someone with that personality type by others simply means that they think that you are annoying. You may feel that you are helpful, but unfortunately, that may not be the case at all. Know-it-all's never really know-it-all. Even if you do know the answer, sometimes it is wise just to be quiet. Instead of listening to your own beat, try listening to the sound that God is playing for you. Use this time to study your niche and craft so that when your time comes, you will know your area of specialty and when called upon by God to operate in it, you are prepared.

Verse of the Day: Listen to my instruction and be wise; do not disregard it. **Proverbs 8:33**

Question of the Day: Are you a know-it-all?/ What is your niche?

_____

_____

_____

_____

_____

Daily Affirmation:

_____

_____

_____

_____

_____

_____

_____

_____

_____

_____

_____

_____

_____

_____

_____

_____

_____

_____

_____

_____

_____

_____

DAY 18

Pamphlet Of Life

When you purchase a product from the store, it comes with instructions, or if you attend an event, you'll receive an order of service. Nowadays, most things come with instructions or a guide, but when you were born, the doctor didn't give your parents an order of service for your life or a manual guide on how to raise you or what would happen in your life year to year. How would you feel if you were given an order of service for your life? If life came with pamphlets, how would things be? Mistakes are what make life so unique and help you learn to become better. The order of service could tell you the exact moment your life will take a turn. Sometimes, we get so caught up in comparing ourselves to others that we overlook the blessing that God has placed upon us. Sometimes, you may feel as if you haven't accomplished much, and you are behind your peers, so you create your pamphlet with a timeline that you think is best for you.

Jeremiah 29:11 states, "For I know the plans I have for you, declares the Lord, plans to prosper you and not to harm you, plans to give you hope and a future." No matter how detailed you think your outline is, it will never be the script God has for you. You can attempt to avoid the route He has for you, but He will bring you right back to your starting point. It may be a thunderstorm right now but remember that storms don't last forever. Your life was uniquely planned. Just because you are at a stop sign in life and it does not seem that you can catch a break, remember that God will always make a way.

Verse of the Day: *For I know the plans I have for you," declares the Lord, "plans to prosper you and not to harm you, plans to give you hope and a future.* **Jeremiah 29:11**

Question of the Day: How would you feel if you were given an order of service for your life?

ANDRE LOVE-HOSEA

Daily Affirmation:

_____

_____

_____

_____

_____

_____

_____

_____

_____

_____

_____

_____

_____

_____

_____

_____

_____

_____

_____

_____

_____

_____

DAY 19

Jump

Do you believe in yourself enough to risk it all for the life you desire, or do you listen to the naysayers and continue to stay in the place you're in now? Your daily routine doesn't change from waking up, working, eating, sleeping, and repeating. Your job pays the bills and supplies you need and want, but when will you get off the edge and take the risk to jump? You owe it to yourself to jump in faith, knowing that God is with you the entire way.

Are you afraid to fail? God shows us tough times before He shows us the most extraordinary times. Being successful doesn't come with a price tag; it comes with happiness. Some of the most successful people are working in a field that they hate and regret not taking the leap to do what they loved when they had the opportunity. If you keep putting off the jump because you are waiting for the perfect time, and there is no such thing, you may miss your window. However, it is not too late to take a chance. Are you in the midst of a jump, or have you already jumped and failed?

Maybe you have asked God for that blessing and wonder why it hasn't come yet, but have you thought that perhaps it's under your feet and you haven't jumped to claim it? Jumping comes with a process that causes bruises and scars from falling and hitting the ground so often, but while you're gaining battle scars, please don't lose hope. The decision to get off the edge is a risk that will be well worth it as God promised to give you life more abundantly, so continue to keep the faith and know that it comes with a greater reward.

Verse of the Day: *The thief does not come except to steal, and to kill, and to destroy. I have come that they may have life, and that they may have it more abundantly.* **John 10:10**

Question of the Day: Why haven't you jumped? Do you believe in God enough to risk it all?

ANDRE LOVE-HOSEA

Daily Affirmation:

_____

_____

_____

_____

_____

_____

_____

_____

_____

_____

_____

_____

_____

_____

_____

_____

_____

_____

_____

_____

_____

_____

DAY 20

50/100

How many times have you gone into something giving it 50% and thinking you would get 100% in return? Thinking as long as you were present, everything is good, but what about participation? You attend church, but are you tithing? You are in the house of the Lord but are you listening to the message? Or maybe you're in class but are you taking notes and listening to the professor? You take the test without studying, hoping that you'll receive a passing grade. You give 50% effort hoping that God gives you double in return, but why is this?

If you aren't giving 100%, what is the point of doing it? Maybe you're satisfied with the results you are receiving from giving 50%. You should try giving your all and see where that lands you. The percentage you give is the same one that God will match. If you are offering 20%, God will do the same. There is a physical fitness test in the military where you are timed 2-minutes on push-ups, sit-ups, and afterward, you are timed for a two-mile run. Suppose I had not worked out the week before testing, how can I expect to demolish the physical fitness test? I can't neglect working out and go to the field, hoping to be a standout. If you put in half the effort, you will get half the return. Each morning you wake up and dedicate 100% to checking your timelines on social media when you should be using that in another area. No matter what you do, make sure to give it your all or simply don't do it. The Bible says Asa was a good king, but he always held back and would never give it his all. Are you like Asa and holding back? I challenge you to give God 100% for the next seven days and watch the outcome.

Verse of the Day: *Were not the Cushites and Libyans a mighty army with great numbers of chariots and horsemen? Yet when you relied on the LORD, he delivered them into your hand. For the eyes of the LORD range throughout the earth to strengthen those whose hearts are fully committed* *to him. You have done a foolish thing, and from now on you will be at war.* **2 Chronicles 16: 8-9**

Question of the Day: In what areas in life do you need to give 100%?

_____
_____
_____
_____
_____
_____
_____
_____
_____
_____
_____
_____
_____
_____
_____
_____
_____
_____
_____
_____
_____

Daily Affirmation:

_____

_____

_____

_____

_____

_____

_____

_____

_____

_____

_____

_____

_____

_____

_____

_____

_____

_____

_____

_____

_____

_____

_____

_____

DAY 21

No Excuses

At the beginning of this journey, you could have made tons of excuses stating why you weren't going to commit to God during this challenge, but you probably realized that decision came with consequences. People make excuses because they don't want to face the consequences. How often do you find yourself attempting to justify things in your life? If you look for an excuse, you will always find one. When you don't make it to your workplace on time, you blame the car or your children for running behind, or when you don't pass your class, you give numerous reasons why you received a particular grade. Instead of driving to work, thinking of several excuses to explain to your supervisor about why you are late, just accept that you will be late, apologize and take the appropriate action to guarantee that you arrive on time.

There is no one to blame for how your life is going right now. If you are looking for someone to blame, then you should go to your nearest mirror and take a good look. We are often quick to name someone else for the wrong things in our life but have you ever sat back and thought maybe it is you? God doesn't give out receipts! You can't return a terrible situation and hope that it turns around; you must take accountability and recognize excuses are for the weak. Life doesn't give you an option to return our bad times for good. We must learn how to take the lemons, add a little sugar, and turn it into a palatable situation. Realize that you control the outcome of YOUR Life. That situation that you are going through now will only prepare you for the greater that God has in store for you, but you will never achieve it if you are creating excuses for why you haven't been able to take advantage of your life.

Verse of the Day: *But thanks be to God, which giveth us the victory through our Lord Jesus Christ.* **1 Cor 15:57**

Question of the Day: Do you take accountability for the things that you have done? Are you looking to blame someone?

Daily Affirmation:

_____

_____

_____

_____

_____

_____

_____

_____

_____

_____

_____

_____

_____

_____

_____

_____

_____

_____

_____

_____

_____

_____

_____

ANDRE LOVE-HOSEA

Andre Love-Hosea, also known as Dre Jose, strives to impact individuals worldwide. He encourages individuals to motivate and mentor others in their sphere of influence. Dre holds a Master Barber license, Bachelor of Science degree from Alabama A&M University, and is currently pursuing a Master of Science in Computer Science. He is a United States Army Officer, founder of Vincent's Hair Studio in Huntsville, Alabama, and co-founder of Studs Incorporated.

He is the son of Angela and Andre Love of Mobile, Alabama. He is a brother of Alpha Phi Alpha Fraternity, Inc., and Men of America Nurturing & Ushering Progress, Inc.

www.ingramcontent.com/pod-product-compliance
Lightning Source LLC
Chambersburg PA
CBHW060441260626
47161CB00005B/2021